This Book Belongs To:

CZ

a gift from:

page ahead
children's literacy program

www.pageahead.org

Oteos, the Elephant of Surprise

IMAGINE & WONDER
Publishers, New York

ISBN: 9781953652218 (HARDCOVER)
ISBN: 9781953652133 (PAPERBACK)
Printed in Canada

Oteos was born,
and raised on the plains.
The others would tease him,
for acting so strange.

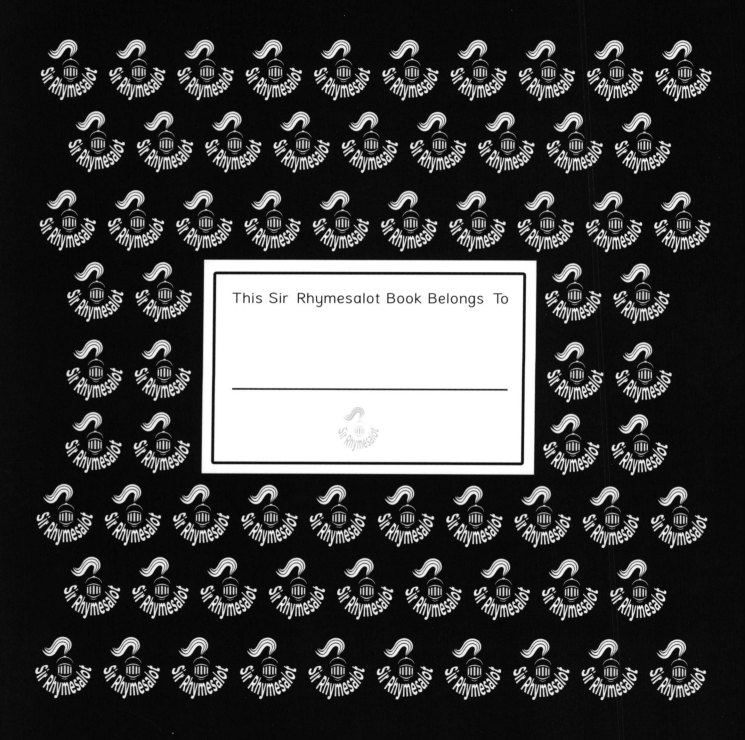

This Sir Rhymesalot Book Belongs To

_____

He knew he was different,
somewhat an "oddie."
He behaved like a squirrel,
with a seven–ton body.

He would hide behind objects,
much smaller than he.
Close his eyes tightly,
so that no one could see.

His friends look away,
and pretend not to notice.
Because they feel sad,
for the odd-acting Oteos.

At parties his mom,
had tears in her eyes.
"But Mom," said Oteos,
"It's just my disguise."

"My friends are in doubt,
the herd don't believe.
But I know I can vanish,
one day they won't see.

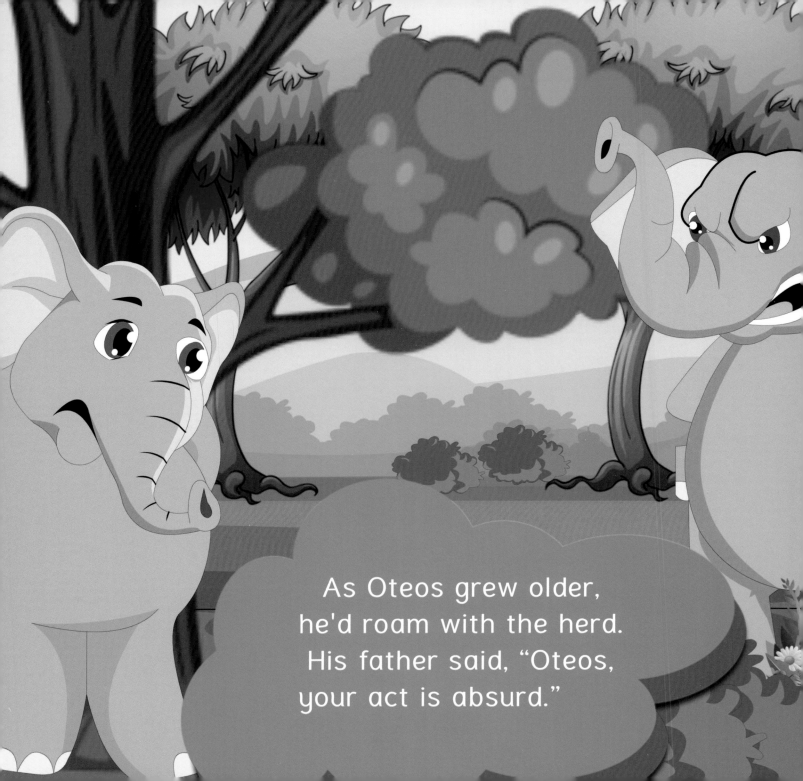

As Oteos grew older,
he'd roam with the herd.
His father said, "Oteos,
your act is absurd."

As the herd gathered food,
they'd watch Oteos hide.
Shaking their heads,
and rolling their eyes.

With tears in his heart,
he left while they slept.
Nobody saw him,
or heard his light steps.

He walked west for days,
then South for miles.
He was terribly lonely,
in his cold, dark exile.

Then far in the distance,
he saw an odd site.
Flames and black smoke,
alight in the night.

His herd could see Oteos,
as they approached from the rear.
Then they saw the big trucks,
they had now come to fear.

The herd didn't know,
what to do or to say.
But Oteos had practiced,
his whole life for this day.

The herd stood frozen,
but Oteos stood tall.
Behind a burnt tree,
that hardly hid him at all.

He attacked from the back.
he really let fly.
Rolling their trucks.
into a canyon nearby.

The hunters had rifles,
but not one shot shot.
With no clue what hit them,
or how they got got.

They could not believe it,
but Oteos was invisible.
He'd saved the whole herd,
but Oteos looked quizzical.

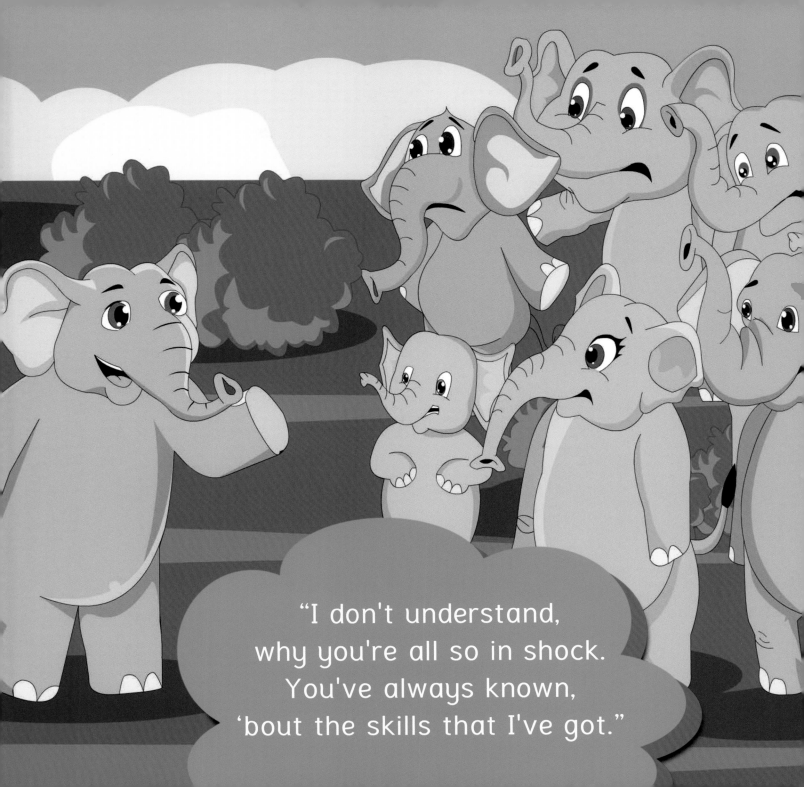

Now the moral of the story,
should your own need arise.
No element is as eloquent,
as the elephant of surprise.

ISBN: 9781953652218 (HARDCOVER)
ISBN: 9781953652133 (PAPERBACK)
Printed in Canada

IMAGINE & WONDER™
Publishers, New York